Disney

Christmas Storybook Collection

PaRRagon

Bath · New York · Singapore · Hong Kong · Cologne · Delhi · Melbourne

First published by Parragon in 2010
Parragon
Queen Street House
4 Queen Street
Bath BA1 1HE, UK

ISBN 978-1-4454-0828-6

Printed in China

Contents

A Toy Christmas

"Take that!" Andy said in Woody's voice. "You're spending Christmas in jail!" He put Hamm the piggy bank into an old shoebox with slits cut into the sides.

Andy was playing in his room with his toys. In one hand he held Woody the cowboy. In the other was Buzz Lightyear the space ranger.

"You'll be seeing bars for a long, long time," Andy added in Buzz Lightyear's commanding tone.

Andy's mother came into the room and sat down on the bed. "Andy, I have a surprise for you," she said. "You know Christmas is coming up. And this year for your big present . . . we're going to the Grand Canyon!"

Andy dropped Woody and Buzz on the floor. He jumped up and down. "Hooray!" Andy said. "That's the best present ever! Can I take Buzz and Woody?" He picked up his two favourite toys.

"I think it's better if you leave them here," his mother said. "You'll be so busy you won't have any time to play. Now come on. We have a lot to do to get ready."

The moment the door shut behind Andy and his mother, the toys came to life. Buzz sat up. Woody straightened his cowboy hat.

"All right!" Rex the dinosaur said as he came out from under the bed. "The trip is Andy's big present this year. That means no other toys to take our places!"

"I was worried Andy was going to get a video game," Hamm added.

All the toys started talking at once.

"Hold on a minute," Woody said. He walked to the centre of the room. "Sure, it's great that there aren't going to be any new toys to replace us. But did you think about what else this means? It means Christmas *without Andy*."

Everyone got quiet. Christmas without Andy? Why, Christmas without Andy wouldn't seem like Christmas at all!

RC's fender drooped sadly. Slinky Dog hung his head. Even the Green Army Men looked glum.

Buzz Lightyear walked over to Woody. "Andy will be gone, but that doesn't mean we can't have Christmas. We'll just make it a toy Christmas!"

Woody looked at the other toys around him. He forced a smile onto his face. "Buzz is right," he said. "We'll have a great Christmas this year."

But deep down, Woody knew it couldn't happen. It was true that they could have their own Christmas. But without the kid who loved them all, it wouldn't be much fun at all.

After Andy and his family left on their trip, the toys started getting ready for Christmas. They had a lot to do. They made decorations, practiced singing songs and looked for presents for each other.

"Psst, Woody, over here," Jessie hissed loudly. Woody found her hiding behind a stack of books. "Look what I found," she said proudly. She held up a red bandanna.

"Why, Jessie, Bullseye has been looking for his bandanna for months!" Woody said.

"I know." Jessie grinned. "It's going to be a great present for him."

"Come sing some Christmas carols," Wheezy the penguin called to Woody.

"All right," Woody said. He thought maybe the songs would put him in the Christmas spirit.

Wheezy grabbed Mike the tape recorder, and as the music began, his high squeaky voice dropped to a deep baritone. First he belted out a rocking rendition of "Santa Claus Is Coming to Town." Then he glided into a jazzy "Frosty the Snowman." But when Wheezy started crooning "Blue Christmas," Woody had to move away. It made him think of how sad he'd be without Andy.

"Catch you later, Wheezy, Mike," Woody said with a tip of his hat.

Wheezy and Mike continued to sing as Woody walked off. He was glad his friends were in the holiday spirit. But he couldn't stop thinking about how much he missed Andy.

He went over to the other side of the room.

"Hey, Woody, want to help us decorate?" Slinky Dog asked. "Watch this." He gave Woody a poke in the ribs, then yelled, "Hit it!" In a flash, two Aliens bounced superhigh and draped a string of red and green buttons along the edge of the bookcase.

"Pretty neat, Slink," Woody said with an approving nod. "And nice job, Sarge," he called to the army commander and his troops. They were hanging sparkly silver jacks that looked like 3-D snowflakes around the room.

"We've got a Christmas tree, too," Slinky Dog told him. He pointed to a tree made entirely of cotton balls. Red and green hair ribbons were wrapped around it and tied into a bow at the top. There already were presents under the tree. They were wrapped in shiny paper and topped with colourful bows.

"Looks like it's a white Christmas," Sarge said.

Woody smiled a little bit. He was impressed that all the toys were working together to make Christmas a happy holiday.

Woody kept track of the days on the calendar in Andy's room. Finally, it was the big one, December 24th. Christmas Eve.

Hours passed with secrets and whispers, and before long, it grew dark outside. The toys all gathered together to celebrate the holiday, but Woody held back. He was thinking of Andy.

"Hey there, Sheriff," Buzz said. "Why so down? It's a beautiful night out there and . . . it's Christmas Eve!"

"I don't know, Buzz," Woody said. "It's just not the same without Andy."

"You're right," Buzz said. "It's not the same. But you have other friends besides Andy. Come on." He put his arm around Woody's shoulders.

Woody and Buzz walked by Bo Peep. She was reading a Christmas story to the newest toys, the ones who had never had a Christmas before. Bo winked at Woody.

Lo and behold, Woody's heart felt a little lighter.

Then, Buzz led Woody over to the Christmas tree. Etch A Sketch stood by the tree, a roaring fire drawn on his screen. Nearby someone had set up the wooden blocks to spell out "MERRY CHRISTMAS."

"Get the lights, Sarge!" Buzz shouted.

The sarge saluted and turned out the lights.

"Here's a little thing I like to call Christmas magic," Buzz said. He pressed the laser button on his right arm, and a beam of red light shot out onto the white wall. He pressed the button again and again and again. It was so quick that his finger became a blur. He moved the lights around – to the right, the left, up, down, left, down, right, up. The light pulsed around the dark room, making a show of dancing snowflakes, sugarplums and lots and lots of toys – dolls, trains, teddy bears.

Woody's jaw dropped and his eyes grew wide. "Wow, Buzz," the cowboy said. "That's really great! I didn't know you could –"

His sentence was cut off
by a jolly "Ho, ho, *rrrrroar!*"
as RC rolled into the circle.
RC was decorated to look like
a sleigh. And following behind
him was Rex with a white cotton
beard and a red sock hat.

"Sorry about the roar," Rex
said, even though no one had
been scared. "Sometimes I forget
I'm Santa Claus, not a fierce bone-crunching carnivorous dinosaur!"

Rex went to the Christmas tree. He picked up presents to give to
each and every toy. Bullseye was thrilled to have his bandanna back.
Mr Spell got brand-new batteries.

"Your speaking was getting a little slow there," Slinky Dog pointed
out.

Buzz got a Star Command four-way outer space signal interceptor. His friends had put it together out of a small cardboard box, some sequins from an old doll dress and lots of duct tape.

"Thanks, guys!" he said. "It's just what I always wanted!"

One of the dolls gave Jessie a dress. Hamm's present was a quarter.

"Woo-hoo," he shouted. "That's as good as twenty-five pennies! Five nickels! Two dimes and a nickel! I'm feeling flush!"

And then Bo Peep pulled Woody over and gave him a big kiss. He turned as red as the Christmas lights. "Aw shucks, Bo," he said.

Woody looked at his friends. Buzz was right. Christmas without Andy wasn't better or worse. It was different. Spending time with people – and toys – you loved was what Christmas was really all about.

"Hey, Buzz, Woody, everyone!" Slinky Dog yelled from the edge of the bed. "Check this out!" He pulled the window curtain aside. Outside, snow drifted down.

"It's a white Christmas!" he shouted. "Merry Christmas, everyone!"

Woody smiled. "Merry Christmas," he replied.

Disney · PIXAR
WALL·E

A Gift for WALL-E

WALL-E and EVE peeked over the top of a pile of rubbish. The humans were acting very strangely. What were they up to now?

They saw two men stringing small coloured lights along a rusty iron fence. Another set up a plastic statue of a fat, white-bearded man in a red suit, red hat and black boots. A woman propped up a fake silver tree and decorated it with shiny red and green glass balls. Now that people had returned to live on Earth along with robots, they were always doing something that surprised WALL-E and EVE. But even for humans they were acting very strangely.

Weirdest of all, the Captain from the Axiom was singing in a loud, joyful voice!

WALL-E and EVE listened to the words carefully. Confused, they looked at each other. Rudolph? A glowing nose? They thought Rudolph must be a kind of robot, like WALL-E and EVE. But neither of them had ever heard of a reindeer-bot before!

WALL-E and EVE snuck closer to where the humans were working. They called their bot friends over. While all the robots watched curiously, the humans hung a green circle with small red dots on a storefront. More of the humans started singing. One small girl even shook a silver ball.

Some of the robots had seen behaviour like this before, when they were living on the spaceship Axiom. It usually happened every twelve months. They had never been able to figure it out.

WALL-E looked closely at the humans. He tried to figure out what made this so different. Then he put his little metal finger on it. The humans looked happy! Most of the time on the Axiom they had looked tired and bored. But there was something about what they were doing right now, here on Earth, that made them very happy.

If it made the humans so happy, WALL-E thought that maybe it would make the robots happy, too!

For hours, the robots studied the humans.
They stored what they had seen in their
computer brains. Next, they set out to copy
the humans.

Some of the bots picked up trash that
the humans had used: bits of tinsel, fake
holly and scraps of brightly coloured paper.

The light bots collected hundreds of
strings of lights. WALL-E already had a
couple in his trailer. He'd always thought
they were pretty, and Eve loved them.
The bots draped WALL-E's trailer with
lights. When the electricity was
turned on, the lights shined so
brightly they looked like a
supernova.

M-O hung up old socks on the other wall. He had no idea why anyone would want to put socks on the wall. But if the humans were doing it, so would he!

The vacuum bot sucked up boxes and boxes of packing peanuts. Unfortunately, he also vacuumed up a nose full of dust. "Ahhhh-chOOOO!" he sneezed. Little white peanuts floated down from the air, coating the floor like a blanket of snow.

WALL-E and EVE roamed the grounds outside the trailer looking for more things to use. WALL-E went one way. EVE went the other.

EVE picked up a piece of shiny metal. She found some scraps of wrapping paper. She stored them inside her chest cavity. Suddenly she heard two humans talking. One of them was the Captain.

"I just love Christmas, don't you?" the other human said. "The lights, the decorations, the cookies, the presents. Christmas is my favourite time of year!"

Christmas! What a lovely word! EVE rolled it around in her mind. It sparked all her circuits. Was this the name for what the humans were doing?

She stopped to listen more closely to what they were saying.

"Yes," said the Captain slowly. "But don't forget, Christmas isn't about things. That's just what Buy-n-Large wants us to believe. It's about *giving*, not just *getting* presents. It's about showing your friends and family that you care."

The Captain's words hummed inside EVE. Robots didn't have family, but they did have friends. And she had one friend who meant more to her than any other – WALL-E. He had come to save her when she was on the ship. He had given her his spare parts. He had cared for her and watched over her. She needed to show him that she appreciated him.

But what kind of a present would do that?

EVE roamed far and wide. She searched and searched. She found many pieces of junk. None of them were quite right. Then, far from WALL-E's trailer, her gaze locked on the perfect present.

A Gift for WALL·E

Two days later, it was Christmas Eve. The bots had prepared a celebration just like the humans'. Some of the smaller bots were stirring with excitement. The umbrella bot wore a pointy red hat with a white pom-pom on top.

The robots beeped out the words to the songs they had heard. They didn't always understand the human words so they made up some of their own.

While all the bots were celebrating the holiday in their own high-tech way, EVE pulled WALL-E aside. She held out a present wrapped in pretty patterned paper.

WALL-E looked surprised. "Ee-vah?" he asked.

EVE nodded.

WALL-E turned the present this way and that. He admired how the shiny paper shimmered in the coloured lights. He was so busy looking at the present that he almost missed EVE motioning to him.

Open it, EVE signalled.

WALL-E carefully unwrapped the present. He folded up each scrap of paper and laid it on the ground next to him. Finally, he pulled away the last piece.

WALL-E held a little evergreen tree in his hands, a miniature Christmas tree.

The longer version of EVE's name was Extraterrestrial Vegetation Evaluator. She had been trained to find plants and was drawn to this little tree. She knew that WALL-E, with his kind ways and big heart, would take care of this present, this living thing, better than anyone.

WALL-E and EVE went outside. Together they dug a hole in the earth and planted the Christmas tree. WALL-E placed a shiny silver star on the top.

WALL-E and EVE looked at the tree. The star twinkled brightly. It reflected the light from the real stars shining in the night sky, far above.

EVE reached out her hand. WALL-E took it. "Ee-vah," he said. Now he understood why humans liked Christmas so much.

WALT DISNEY'S
MICKEY MOUSE

Mickey's
Christmas Carol

It was snowing in London, England, on Christmas Eve. Ebenezer Scrooge, the richest man in town, hurried towards his office.

"Merry Christmas!" someone shouted.

"Bah, humbug," Scrooge muttered. He didn't know why everyone had to be so cheerful at Christmas time. When Scrooge reached the door to his office, he looked up at the sign. It read SCROOGE & MARLEY. But Marley's name was crossed out. He'd been dead for seven years.

Scrooge and Jacob Marley had tricked people who didn't have much into giving them money. They had gotten very rich and hadn't cared that they'd been unfair. Scrooge cackled as he thought of all his money.

44

Bob Cratchit, Scrooge's clerk, was just about to throw a piece of coal into the stove when Scrooge walked in.

"What are you doing?" Scrooge growled.

"I was just trying to thaw out the ink," Bob replied. He gave his boss a small but hopeful smile.

Scrooge knocked the coal out of Bob's hand and scowled. "You used a piece last week! Get back to work," he said.

Bob quickly turned back to his desk.

After a few moments, Bob snuck a glance at his boss. Then he said, "Speaking of work, Mr Scrooge . . . tomorrow is Christmas. And I was just wondering if . . . if I might have the day off?"

Scrooge was silent for a long time. "Very well," he finally said. "But make sure you come in early the day after!"

Scrooge hung up his jacket and hat. Then he sat down at his desk and began to count his money. "Heh, heh, heh . . . money, money, money!" he crowed.

Suddenly, the door burst open. A young man carrying a wreath walked in.

"Merry Christmas!" the man said. It was Scrooge's nephew Fred.

"Christmas?" Scrooge scoffed. "Bah, humbug!"

Fred walked up to Scrooge's desk and gave him the wreath. He thought the office could use some holiday cheer.

"Uncle, I've come to invite you to Christmas dinner tomorrow," Fred said with a smile.

Scrooge hurried inside and up to his bedroom. He closed the door and climbed into his chair. He heard the sounds of clanking chains. He shivered, too afraid to move.

Then a ghost appeared beside him! It was Jacob Marley. He was covered in heavy chains.

"Ebeneeezer," the ghost wailed. He rattled his chains. "Do you know who I am?"

Scrooge peered at the ghost from under his top hat.

"When I was alive, I robbed from widows and took money from the poor," Jacob said.

"You were a fine partner, Jacob," Scrooge said with a smile.

"No!" Jacob replied. "I was wrong. And now I have to carry these chains forever as punishment. The same thing will happen to you. Tonight, you will be visited by three spirits. If you don't listen to them, your chains will be heavier than mine."

Then Jacob's ghost disappeared.

Scrooge was still shaking with fear as he got ready for bed. After checking his room for more ghosts, he climbed under the covers. "Humbug," he muttered. Then he fell asleep.

But it wasn't long before a noise woke him up. *Ding! Ding! Ding!* His clock bell was ringing. Scrooge opened his eyes to find a little cricket in a top hat on his bedside table.

"I am the Ghost of Christmas Past," the cricket said. "We're going to visit your past tonight."

The ghost went to the window and pushed it open.

"Just hold on," the ghost said as he hopped into Scrooge's hand.

Scrooge did as the cricket said, and they flew out into the darkness.

The city passed slowly beneath them as they flew high above snow-covered rooftops.

The first stop Scrooge and the Ghost of Christmas Past made was at a little shop. A party was taking place inside.

Scrooge looked through the window.

"It's old Fezziwig's!" he exclaimed. He saw his old boss and many of his dearest friends laughing and dancing inside.

Then he saw Isabelle, the girl he had once loved. She was dancing with a young man. It was him – back before he had become a greedy old man.

As if reading Scrooge's mind, the ghost said, "In ten years' time, you learned to love something else much more."

The spirit showed Scrooge another scene. Isabelle and Scrooge were in his counting house.

"Ebenezer," Isabelle said softly, "have you made a decision about getting married?"

"I have," Scrooge replied. "The last payment on your cottage was late." Then he told her he was taking the cottage away.

Isabelle began to cry.

As Scrooge watched, he shook his head.

"Remember, Scrooge," the ghost said. "You made these memories."

Scrooge found himself back in his bed again. Then he heard a loud voice say, "I am the Ghost of Christmas Present."

Scrooge looked up and saw a giant. The giant lifted him up and carried him out into the night. He brought Scrooge to a shabby little house. Through the window, Scrooge saw Bob Cratchit with his family. They were having Christmas dinner.

On the table sat the smallest bird Scrooge had ever seen. "Surely they have more food than that," he whispered.

Then a smaller boy hobbled into the room on a crutch. His name was Tiny Tim.

Tiny Tim looked at the meal on the table. "We must thank Mr Scrooge!" he exclaimed.

Scrooge turned around to ask about Tiny Tim, but the ghost was gone. He was all alone in a graveyard. Suddenly, he saw a dark figure.

"Are you the Ghost of Christmas Future?" Scrooge asked.

The ghost was silent. He pointed to a gravestone.

Scrooge saw the Cratchit family without Tiny Tim. They were near his grave, crying.

The spirit pointed to an empty pit.

"Whose lonely grave is this?" Scrooge asked. Then he realized it was his.

"I can change!" Scrooge cried. "Let me change!"

Suddenly, Scrooge was in his bed again. He ran to the window and looked outside. The sun was shining. The streets were covered with snow. Christmas bells were ringing.

"It's Christmas morning!" he cried. "The spirits have given me another chance!"

He pulled on his hat and coat and ran outside. "Merry Christmas!" he called to everyone he passed.

He saw his nephew, Fred, on the street. "I'm looking forward to that wonderful meal of yours!" he called as he ran by.

Bob Cratchit heard a loud knock on his front door. He opened it to find Mr Scrooge on the step, holding a large bag.

Scrooge dumped the sack on the floor. Dozens of toys fell out. Scrooge smiled as the children rushed forward happily.

"Bob Cratchit," Scrooge said, "I'm giving you a raise and making you my partner!"

Then he handed a large turkey to Mrs Cratchit.

"Merry Christmas!" he said happily.

"Merry Christmas to us all," said Tiny Tim.

Disney
Winnie the Pooh
THE SWEETEST CHRISTMAS

One snowy Christmas Eve, Winnie the Pooh looked up and down, in and out and all around his house.

He had a tree set up in his living room. It was decorated with some candles in honey pots.

Pooh looked at the tree and tapped his head. "Something seems to be missing," he said.

He walked over to the window and peered outside. Then he walked back to the tree and thought some more.

Suddenly, a knocking sound startled Pooh. *Rap-a-tap-tap!* He turned towards his front door.

"Maybe whatever it is I can't remember I'm missing is outside my door," Pooh said.

When Pooh opened the door, he found a small snowman on his front step.

"H-h-he-l-l-l-o, P-Pooh B-Bear," the snowman said as he shivered.

Pooh thought the voice sounded very familiar. He invited the snowman inside.

After standing beside the fire for a few minutes, the snowman began to melt. The more he melted, the more he started to look like Piglet!

"Oh, my," said Pooh. He was happy to see his friend where there used to be a snowman.

"Oh, my," said Piglet. Now that the snow had melted off him, he could see Pooh's glowing Christmas tree.

"Are you going to string popcorn for your tree?" Piglet asked.

"There was popcorn and string," Pooh admitted. "But now there is only string."

Pooh thought some more, wondering if popcorn was what he'd forgotten. But that wasn't it, either.

"Then we can use the string to wrap the presents you're giving," Piglet said.

Something began to tickle at Pooh's brain. It was the something missing that he hadn't been able to remember.

"I forgot to get presents!" Pooh exclaimed.

"Don't worry, Pooh," Piglet said. "I'm sure you'll think of something."

Soon it was time for Piglet to go home and wrap his own presents. He said good-bye to his friend and went back out into the cold, snowy night.

Pooh stood beside his tree and tapped his head while he thought. Where could he find presents for his friends? It was already Christmas Eve. Was it too late?

He thought some more. He sat down in his cozy chair. Then he got up and had a small snack of honey. He peered out the window and watched the snow fall.

Then he had an idea.

He still didn't know what to do about the presents he'd forgotten. But he knew where to find help.

"Hello!" Pooh called as he knocked on Christopher Robin's door.

Christopher Robin opened the door and smiled when he saw the visitor. "Come in, Pooh Bear," he said. "Merry Christmas! Why do you look so sad on the most wonderful night of the year?"

Pooh was just about to explain about the forgotten presents when something caught his eye. He pointed at the stockings over the fireplace. "What are those for?" he asked.

"Those are stockings to hold Christmas presents," explained Christopher Robin.

"But Christopher Robin," Pooh said, "what if someone forgot to find presents for his friends? And what if that same someone doesn't have stockings to hang because he doesn't wear any?"

Pooh looked down at his bare feet, then back up at Christopher Robin.

"Silly old bear," Christopher Robin said. He took Pooh up to his room. They dug through his drawers until Pooh found seven stockings.

"Thank you, Christopher Robin," Pooh said. He smiled. He'd picked a stocking for each of his friends to put their presents in: purple for Piglet, red-and-white striped for Tigger, orange for Rabbit, yellow for Eeyore, maroon for Gopher, and blue for Owl. And one for him to hang over his fireplace.

He hurried off to deliver the stockings to his friends. As he walked through the Hundred-Acre Wood, he thought about the presents he still needed for the stockings.

"I will get the presents later," Pooh said to himself. "The stockings come first."

Pooh stopped at each of his friends' houses. Everyone was asleep. He quietly hung the stockings where his friends would find them. Each one had a tag that read: FROM POOH.

When Pooh got back to his house, he climbed into his cozy chair in front of a roaring fire.

"Now I must think about presents for my friends," he said.

But Pooh was tired from finding the stockings and delivering them to his friends' houses. Before he knew it, his thinking turned into dreaming. He was fast asleep.

The next morning, Pooh awoke to a loud thumping noise.

Thump-a-bump-bump!

"I wonder who that could be," he said. He climbed out of his chair and opened the door.

"Merry Christmas, Pooh!" his friends cried.

There on Pooh's doorstep stood Tigger, Rabbit, Piglet, Owl, Eeyore and Gopher. They were each carrying the stocking from Pooh.

Pooh scratched his head. All of a sudden he remembered what had happened the night before. He had fallen asleep before giving presents to his friends!

"Oh, bother," he said. Then he realized that his friends were all talking at once. They were thanking him for their gifts!

"No more cold ears in the winter with my new cap," Piglet said.

"My stripedy sleeping bag is tigger-ific!" exclaimed Tigger.

"So is my new carrot cover," Rabbit said.

"This rock-collecting bag will sure make work go faster," Gopher said.

Eeyore swished his tail to show Pooh his new tail-warmer. "No one's ever given me such a useful gift before," he said.

Owl told Pooh his new wind sock would help him with the day's weather report.

Pooh looked at his friends. They were very happy with their stockings, even though there weren't any presents in them!

"Something very nice is going on," Pooh said.

"It is very nice, Pooh Bear," Piglet said.

"It's called Christmas, buddy bear," Tigger said. He patted Pooh on the back.

Then, Pooh watched in surprise as each of his friends put a honey pot in his own stocking.

"I don't know what to say," Pooh told his friends. He was thrilled by their gifts. Honey was his favourite treat!

"Christmas is a wonderful holiday," Rabbit said. "Especially when you have good friends to share it with."

"Yep!" Tigger agreed. "But I know how we could make the day even sweeter."

He looked at the honey pot in Pooh's hands.

An idea tickled at Pooh's brain. "Let's all have lunch together," Pooh said. He passed out the honey pots his friends had just brought him. "Christmas . . . what a sweet day, indeed."

Bambi

The Wonderful Winter Tree

Bambi awoke one morning to find the whole world covered in a soft white blanket.

"What is it, Mother?" Bambi asked as he gazed around in wonder.

"This is snow," replied his mother. "It means winter is upon us."

"Snow!" said Bambi. He took a cautious step . . . and then another . . . and another. He felt the icy crystals crunch under his hooves. He looked back at the tiny tracks he had made. "I *like* snow!" Bambi said.

"Snow is pretty to look at," his mother told him, "but it makes winter hard for all the animals."

Bambi was about to ask her why winter was harder than other seasons. But just then, his friend Thumper came hopping over.

"Hiya, Bambi!" said the bunny. "Come on! Let's go sliding!" He led Bambi to the pond, which was frozen solid.

Thumper slapped at the ice with his foot. "Come on! It's all right," he told Bambi. "See! The water's stiff!"

Bambi saw his friend, Flower the skunk.

"You want to come sliding?" Bambi called, running over. "Thumper says the water's stiff."

But Flower shook his head. "No thanks. I'm off to my den. I'm going to sleep through the winter." He yawned. "Good-bye, Bambi," he said.

"'Bye, Flower," said Bambi. Then he spied another friend, a squirrel, scurrying up an oak tree.

"The pond is stiff, Squirrel," called Bambi. "Want to come sliding with me?"

"Thanks," replied the squirrel as he ducked into a hollow in the tree, "but I have to store nuts for the long winter." He showed Bambi the pile he had already collected. "No sliding for me today."

So Bambi headed back to Thumper and the ice-covered pond by himself.

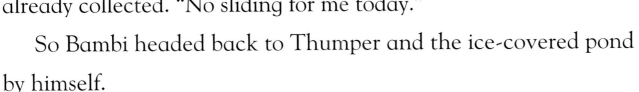

By that time, Thumper was sliding across the ice with some of his sisters. They made it look so easy. But when Bambi stepped on the ice, he lost his balance right away. His hooves went sliding in four different directions!

"Kind of wobbly, aren't ya," said Thumper. He laughed. "Come on, Bambi. You can do it!"

But Bambi wasn't so sure. Sliding across the stiff water wasn't quite as much fun for deer, it seemed, as it was for rabbits. And it also made him hungry. He said good-bye to the bunnies and went back to find his mother.

"Mother, I'm hungry," Bambi told her.

In the spring, summer and autumn, they had been able to find food almost anywhere they looked. But now that it was winter, Bambi could see that finding food wasn't so easy. There were no leaves on the trees, and the grass was covered with snow and ice. The snow was so cold that when he poked through it, Bambi thought his nose might freeze.

At last Bambi's mother uncovered a small patch of grass. Bambi nibbled it eagerly.

Then Bambi curled up with his mother for a nap. The ground was hard and cold and the wind was chilly. Bambi was grateful to have his mother there to keep him warm.

"Is this why the birds fly south and why our other friends sleep through the winter?" Bambi asked her.

His mother nodded and snuggled even closer. "But don't worry, Bambi," she told him. "Winter doesn't last forever."

By the end of December, there seemed nothing left in the forest but bitter bark for Bambi to eat. The days grew short and the nights grew long, and throughout them Bambi's stomach rumbled. And then one day, something truly amazing happened.

Thumper was the first to see it. "Hey, Bambi!" he hollered. "Would you look at that tree!"

Bambi followed Thumper's paw. He could not believe his eyes.

There before them was a tall pine tree unlike any Bambi had ever seen. It was draped with strings of bright berries and yummy popcorn, and from the end of each branch hung 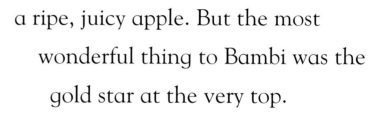 a ripe, juicy apple. But the most wonderful thing to Bambi was the gold star at the very top.

"Mother!" exclaimed Bambi. "Look what Thumper found!"

Slowly and cautiously, his mother drew closer. "It can't be . . ." she whispered. "It seems almost too good to be true."

"What *is* it, Mother?" Bambi asked her.

"The most beautiful tree in the world," she answered. She smiled down at Bambi. "What a special gift to have on your first Christmas."

"Who left it, Mother?" Bambi asked.

"I don't know," she replied.

"Maybe someone who loves animals," Thumper said, hopping up and down. "This is the best gift ever." He sniffed one of the apples hanging low to the ground.

"Can we share this food with every one of our friends, Mother?" Bambi asked.

"Yeah, and with my sisters, too?" Thumper chimed in.

"I don't see why not," Bambi's mother said. "Christmas is a time to share what we have with those we love."

Bambi and Thumper danced happily around the tree. "Look at all the popcorn and berries!" Thumper cried. "And look at that star at the tippy-top, too!"

Bambi stopped prancing. He looked up at the golden star at the top of the tree. Then he looked up at the sky above him. The sun was just beginning to go down. He knew that very soon, there would be a star twinkling in the sky just like the one at the top of the tree. A gentle hush fell over the clearing.

He danced back over to his mother and took a big bite out of one of the juicy green apples. *Mmm!* he thought. Nothing had ever tasted so good!

Gazing up at the star and at the wonderful winter tree, Bambi could feel a happy, warm glow swelling inside him. There was enough food on the tree to feed all the animals who were hungry. What a magical gift, thought Bambi. Winter *was* long and hard . . . and yet wonderful, after all.

WALT DISNEY'S

Snow White
and the Seven Dwarfs

A Christmas
to Remember

Once upon a time, a princess named Snow White had to run away from her evil stepmother's castle. She happened upon a cozy cottage in the woods that belonged to the Seven Dwarfs. When the Dwarfs heard that Snow White's life was in danger, they insisted she stay with them. After several months, they thought of each other like family.

One December morning, Snow White was out feeding the birds and her other forest friends. Doc sat down with the other Dwarfs. "Christmas is coming," he said. "What do you say we give Snow White a gifty nift – er – a nifty gift!"

"We need to show our appreciation for all she's done for us," said Happy.

"Aw, why not! She deserves something, I guess," said Grumpy.

Sleepy said, "She could use a new quilt for her bed."

"How about a lace handkerchief?" suggested Sneezy.

"I have an idea," said Bashful, blushing. "Why not give her something from our mines? Something for her to remember us by?"

"Remember us? She's not going anywhere," said Grumpy. "Is she?"

"Let's hope not." Sleepy yawned.

"If we work extra hard," said Doc, "we could find the perfect piamond – er – diamond."

"We could make her a crown," said Happy. "A crown like a princess would wear."

"Snow White *is* a princess," Bashful reminded them.

The next day the Dwarfs busied themselves at the mine. They wanted to be sure they found the perfect gift.

In the cottage, Snow White got ready for Christmas, too. First, she made a tray of special cookies, cutting them into the shapes of bells and stars and Christmas trees.

While the cookies baked, she went into the forest and cut down a dwarf-sized pine tree. She pulled it home on a small sled, gathering red berries and holly leaves along the way.

"It's a beautiful surprise," said Happy.

"We have a little surprise for you, too," Doc added. He took a small package wrapped in brown paper out of his cloak and

placed it under the tree. "No squeaking – er – peeking," he said.

"Please wait until Christmas Eve," Bashful added shyly.

Snow White was surprised. "You didn't have to give me a present," she said. "You've already been so kind to me."

On Christmas Eve, Snow White cooked a feast of roast fowl
and a delicious cake. All night, she kept looking at the package
beneath the tree. Her stepmother, the evil Queen, had never given
her anything. This was her very first Christmas present.

At last, the meal was finished, and the Dwarfs had washed all of the dishes. Doc handed Snow White the small bundle.

When she opened it, Snow White gasped with delight. "Why, this is lovely! But how did you ever . . . ?"

"We made it," said Happy proudly.

Snow White went to the mirror and put on the crown.

"Oh, thank you," she said. "This is wonderful – and it is even more precious because you put your hearts into it."

"Shucks, it wasn't much," said Bashful.

"But it is," Snow White cried. "You've made my first Christmas very memorable."

Snow White wore the splendid crown all through the Christmas holiday. Then she wrapped it carefully and tucked it away. She wanted to keep her beautiful gift ready for the next time she wore it.

Lady's Christmas Surprise

It was the week before Christmas. Tramp and the puppies gathered beneath Jim and Darling's brightly decorated tree.

"You all know what holiday is coming up, right?" Tramp asked, his eyes twinkling.

"Of course, Dad," Scamp said. He was excited. Christmas was the puppies' favourite holiday. Lots of guests stopped by to wish Jim and Darling a happy holiday.

But the best part was the presents. The puppies got to help choose a special gift for each of their parents. They loved being trusted with two such important surprises.

"Do any of you kids know what your mother would like for Christmas?" Tramp asked.

"How about a steak from Tony's Restaurant?" Annette said.

Tramp shook his head. "We can do better than that."

"We need to give her something special," said Colette, "to show how much we love her."

"Why don't you ask her what she'd like?" said Scamp, his voice muffled. He was chewing on a bow.

"We want to surprise her," Tramp reminded his son. He nudged him away from the presents. "That's the fun of Christmas."

"Maybe we'll find something on our walk today," Annette said.

Tramp thought that was a good idea. While Lady was taking a nap, he took the kids into town to look for the perfect present.

The village bustled with shoppers, their carriage wheels carving deep ruts in the snowy road.

The dogs rambled up and down the avenue, looking in all the shop windows. They saw sweaters, cushions, brush and comb sets, bowls and collars. But Tramp knew that none of these things was the perfect gift for Lady. He wanted to find her something special. Something that she would enjoy and that no other dog would have.

Tramp and the puppies kept looking into store windows and they peeked at the packages people carried. All they needed was one really good idea.

When the sun started to sink in the sky, Tramp turned to the puppies and said, "We'd better head for the alleys and dig something from the trash."

As they crossed the road, Tramp noticed something sparkling in the snow. It was much brighter than an icicle. He turned it over with his paw.

"Holy hambones!" he cried. It was a gold and diamond necklace!

"What a bunch of rocks!" exclaimed Scamp.

"What a good stroke of luck!" remarked Annette.

"Just the right size for Mother!" added Colette.

Tramp smiled and then scooped up the necklace with his mouth. They'd found the perfect gift. He knew it would look beautiful on Lady.

Suddenly, Tramp dropped the necklace into the snow. It sparkled in the icy crystals. He frowned.

"What's the matter?" Scamp asked.

"This isn't right," Tramp muttered. Then he looked at his children. "Sorry, kids, but we have to return the necklace. It's not ours to take."

"But where would we go to return it?" Colette asked.

"Yeah, it was just here in the snow," Annette said. "How would we even find the owner?"

"I say finders keepers!" Scamp cried.

"Come on now, kids," Tramp said. "We can take it to the police. They'll know who to return it to."

With the puppies following, he bounded down the block to the station.

Inside, officers hurried around taking phone calls and writing reports.

"Stay close, kids," Tramp whispered to the puppies. "I don't want to lose you in the crowd."

Tramp trotted up to the front desk, the puppies following behind. He dropped the necklace in front of the policeman in charge.

"What's this?" the officer said as he looked at the dog and then back to the necklace on the desk. He picked up the necklace and looked at the sparkling jewels.

Tramp panted and wagged his tail. The puppies stood eagerly beside him. *Yip! Yip!*

"You found it?" the officer asked.

Tramp nodded.

"Good dog!" he exclaimed.

The policeman took the necklace and began filling out his report while Tramp and the puppies watched.

At that moment, a woman rushed into the station. "Help!" she cried. "My necklace is gone! I'm offering a reward for its return."

The policeman smiled at the woman. Then he held out the necklace. "Is this yours?" he asked. He pointed to Tramp. "This dog found it on the street and brought it here."

The woman gasped. "Thank you," she said. She scratched Tramp behind his ear. "How can I repay you?"

Woof! Tramp looked at the necklace.

"A new collar," she said. "That's it!"

She took Tramp and the puppies to the shop next door. Tramp walked up to the counter and picked up a gold collar with green stones that looked just like the woman's necklace.

"I'll take that one," the woman told the shopkeeper.

On Christmas morning Lady tore open the gift. "You shouldn't have!" Her eyes sparkled like the green stones.

When Darling fastened the collar around Lady's neck, she pranced around the room as if she were a show dog.

"I love my new collar," Lady said. "What a wonderful Christmas surprise! But I love my family even more." She nuzzled Tramp and each of the puppies.

"Merry Christmas, Mother," said the puppies.

And it was a very merry Christmas, indeed.

Disney's
Beauty and the Beast
The Enchanted Christmas

Winter had settled over the castle grounds. Belle looked out the window at the snow-covered trees. She tried to make the best of those cold, wintry days, but she was sad. Christmas would be here soon, and she wished she could be home to celebrate with her father. As long as she was a prisoner in the Beast's castle, she was forbidden to leave the grounds.

Then she had a wonderful idea. She could celebrate Christmas at the castle with her new friends! She hurried off to find them and share her plans.

"Out of the question!" Cosgworth the clock said when Belle told him her idea. "The master has forbidden Christmas."

Belle couldn't believe what she was hearing. "No one can forbid Christmas! I, for one, think a little Christmas cheer would do him much good."

"The girl is right," agreed Lumiere the candelabra. "It is up to us to do something."

Cogsworth was still unsure. But as soon as Belle mentioned Christmas pudding, the clock changed his mind.

"If the master finds out about this, he will be furious," warned Cogsworth. "So everybody, keep quiet!"

The surprise didn't last long, though. When the Beast found out, he growled with anger. "I hate Christmas," he roared to Forte the pipe organ. Forte was the only one who understood how upset the Beast had been since the curse had been placed upon the Castle.

The Beast had once been a handsome prince. But one day he had refused to offer help to an old woman. When she saw his selfishness, she turned him into a beast and all of his servants into enchanted objects.

Before the magical curse, Forte had been the court composer. None of the other servants had liked him or his music, but they had always listened politely. Now that the Beast was unhappy, Forte could play sad songs all the time. The Beast often came and sat by the fire and listened to the music. Forte liked that he was important to the master. He didn't want this to change.

Next, it was time to find a Yule log. Belle went to the boiler room and looked around. Finally, she found one she liked.

Just then, the Beast stormed into the room. He snatched the log out of her hands.

"It's a Yule log," Belle said. "It's a wonderful tradition. Everyone in the house touches it and makes a Christmas wish."

"Wishes are stupid," growled the Beast. "You made a Christmas wish last year. Is this what you wished for?"

"No," Belle replied. "But I will keep wishing. And when the log is burned on Christmas morning –"

"There will be no Christmas!" insisted the Beast. "I am the master here!"

Belle was upset, but she decided to continue with her Christmas plans. The next morning, she and Chip set out to find a tree. They were looking for one that was tall and wide. But all the trees near the castle were too skinny or too small.

Belle had brought along an ax just in case. She decided to bring back one of the small trees. It would have to do if she couldn't find anything else.

When Belle returned to the castle, she heard Forte playing his music. She went to see him.

Forte didn't like Belle. He wanted to get rid of her so the witch's curse would never be lifted. That meant he would always get to play his sad music.

The organ asked Belle how the Christmas plans were coming. Belle told him that she wished she could find the perfect tree to decorate. Forte told her to go into the Black Forest, even though he knew it wasn't safe.

Belle looked out the window. The dark forest was in the distance. "It looks dangerous," she said.

"Mademoiselle, you are in more danger in this very room, I assure you," Forte lied.

Belle agreed to go into the forest and soon set off in her sleigh. After she left, Forte ordered Fife the flute to follow her. He wanted to make sure she didn't come back!

A little later, the Beast began to look around the castle for Belle. He couldn't find her anywhere. He looked in his enchanted mirror. "Show me the girl!" he ordered. In the mirror, he saw Belle riding through the forest. He was furious.

Forte tried to convince the Beast that he was better off without her, but it was no use. His master was not ready to let the girl go. The Beast went after Belle, determined to bring her back.

In the forest, Belle and Chip found the perfect tree. They tied it to the back of the sleigh with a rope.

But Fife was lurking in the forest. He made a high-pitched sound that caused Belle's horse to rear back in fear as the sleigh crossed a frozen pond. The horse broke loose from the sleigh. *Crack!* The ice began to separate.

Belle gasped as the teacup and the tree fell into the water. With a deep breath, she dove in and grabbed hold of Chip. She swam to the surface and put the little teacup safely on land. But Belle was pulled back under the water by the rope from the tree.

Luckily, the Beast arrived at that moment. He dove into the water just in time and saved Belle.

Forte was angry about the way things had turned out. "So Beast gets the girl, and it's a happy ending for everyone," he muttered. "Enchantment lifted, and Forte fades into the background. No longer important, no longer needed . . . I think not!"

The jealous organ blasted his music throughout the castle. The walls shook, and windows shattered.

"Forte! Enough!" the Beast commanded.

The organ wouldn't listen, though. He kept playing. "Is this happy enough for you, Master?" Forte said.

Finally, the Beast did the only thing he could. He smashed the keyboard. The music ended.

Forte tried to play his notes but no sound came out. He angrily tore himself away from the wall. The evil organ crumbled and broke into many pieces, never to play again.

Everyone was relieved that Forte wouldn't be around anymore. Now happy music could play throughout the castle.

On Christmas Day, the Beast escorted Belle into the main hall. The whole castle had been beautifully decorated, and everyone was full of good cheer.

It was a Christmas no one would ever forget, especially the Beast. For on that day, Belle gave him the gift of hope – the hope that someday the curse would be lifted and life in the castle would return to normal.

A Big Blue Christmas

"Dad, wake up!" Nemo shouted early one morning as he swam back and forth across their anemone home.

"What is it, Nemo?" asked Marlin, waking in a hurry. "Are you hurt? Is something wrong?"

"No, Dad," the little clownfish answered. "It's just that I have a terrific idea! It's almost Christmas. Could we have a holiday party?"

"Sounds like fun, Nemo," Marlin said with a yawn. "But let's wait until after breakfast to start planning."

Right after breakfast, Nemo and Marlin made a list of friends to invite. It was a long list because they had friends all over the ocean. Marlin wondered how they'd let everyone know in time.

"I can ask Bruce, Chum and Anchor to help spread the word," Nemo offered. "No one can say 'no' to those guys."

Marlin thought it over. Nemo was right. No fish he knew wanted to get on a shark's bad side. "Well, all right, son," he said. "But be careful."

"I know, Dad," Nemo said. "See you later!" he called as he swam off.

Nemo swam as fast as he could to the old shipwreck where his shark friends hung out. "Hey, Bruce! Guys!" Nemo said when he arrived.

"Check out what the tide washed in," said Anchor.

"Why it's our little food – I mean friend – Nemo," Chum said.

"What brings you out this way, Nemo?" asked Bruce.

The little clownfish told them all about the Christmas party. The sharks were thrilled. They hadn't been asked to many parties. Then Nemo asked them to help tell everyone about it.

"You can count on us," Bruce said proudly.

"Thanks," said Nemo. "And, guys, we will be counting our guests, too, so remember . . ."

"Fish are friends, not food," the four of them said together.

Nemo swam home as fast as he could. His father was swimming back and forth across their anemone nervously.

"We need to plan the menu," Marlin muttered. "And then there's cleaning and decorating and . . ."

"Stop right there, Dad," said Nemo. "We're going to need help. I'll be back later with more fins!"

Nemo had made some great friends when he had been captured and put in a tank in a dentist's office in Sydney. The whole Tank Gang had eventually escaped and were now living in the ocean.

Next, Nemo swam off to find their friend Dory, the regal blue tang fish.

"Do I know you?" Dory asked when Nemo finally found her. Nemo smiled. Dory was the most forgetful fish he knew. All of a sudden, Dory hugged him and said, "Memo! I've missed you!"

"Would you like to help us decorate for a party?" said Nemo.

"I *love* parties," said Dory. "At least I think I love parties. I can't really remember if I've ever been to one."

That afternoon, Dory, Marlin and Nemo worked hard putting up all the decorations. They hung streamers and wreaths and decorated a conch-shell Christmas tree.

Meanwhile, the sharks were busy inviting all the guests. Finally, just the sea turtles were left. The three sharks took a ride on the East Australian Current to catch up with them. "Hey, shark dudes, Marlin asked us to invite you to a holiday party back at their anemone." Bruce said.

"Awesome," said Crush. "I love to party!"

Squirt popped out from underneath Crush's back flipper. "Hey, dudes, can I come, too?"

"Of course," said Chum. "Nemo wants all his foods – I mean, friends – there."

"Cool!" said Squirt.

Back at the anemone, there was only one more detail left to plan. A good party needed great music. That gave Nemo an idea.

Nemo went to see his friends Tad the butterfly fish, Sheldon the sea horse, and Pearl the squid.

"Hi, Nemo," said Sheldon.

"Hi, guys," Nemo said. "Guess what? My dad and I are having a holiday party. But we need a band. I thought we could play!"

"Cool," said Pearl. "I've been humming 'Jingle Shells' all day!"

"Let's practice right now," added Tad. He grabbed some kelp and started to strum.

Pearl joined in on the sand-dollar tambourines. Sheldon kept the beat on the clams. This made the clams pretty cranky!

Then Nemo joined in on the conch shell on the second verse.

They practiced all afternoon.

"We'll be great!" Nemo said when they finished. They sounded really good. "See you at the party!"

Finally, the night of the party arrived! Wearing colourful Christmas sea garlands, Marlin and Nemo greeted their guests. Seeing all of his friends together filled Nemo with holiday cheer.

"Welcome to our party," Marlin said to Crush and Squirt.

"Merry Christmas!" Nemo said to Dory and the sharks.

"Thanks," said Dory as she swam past. "I just ran into these guys, and they told me there was a party over here tonight. Hey, these decorations look amazing. Who did them?"

"Dory, you helped me decorate for the party," Nemo said.

"I did?" asked Dory. "Wow, I'm good."

Before long, the party was filled with friends from near and far. Deb's seaweed-and-kelp cake was delicious. There was even ginger-kelp fish decorating the top of the cake. Everyone loved that best of all. The guests washed their treats down with salty seawater punch. Everyone was gathered around the conch-shell Christmas tree having a great time.

After all the presents were opened, Nemo decided it was time for some live music.

"C'mon, guys," Nemo whispered to Pearl, Sheldon and Tad. "Time to get everyone singing and dancing."

And they did! The guests all turned to watch as Nemo, Sheldon, Tad and Pearl started to play "We Wish You a Merry Fishmas."

Mr Ray, Nemo's teacher, sang along loudly. Even the sharks flipped their fins to the beat.

The party really got swinging as the band played more Christmas carols.

In between songs, Deb swam over to Nemo. "Great party," Deb said. "Your dad is such a nice guy. Isn't it wonderful being able to travel the big wide ocean to visit friends?"

"You bet, Deb!" Nemo answered. He slapped fins with his friend. "Fish aren't meant to live in a tank."